W9-DHK-607

THE LITTLE ENGINE THAT COULD™

The Complete Original

Retold by Watty Piper

Illustrated by George & Doris Hauman

Publishers • PLATT & MUNK • *New York*
A Division of Grosset & Dunlap

1990 Miniature Edition

Copyright © 1976, 1961, 1954, 1945, 1930 by Platt & Munk, Publishers. All rights reserved.
Published by Platt & Munk, Publishers, an imprint of Grosset & Dunlap, which is a division of
Penguin Young Readers Group, 345 Hudson Street, New York, NY 10014.
THE LITTLE ENGINE THAT COULD, engine design, I THINK I CAN, and
PLATT & MUNK are trademarks of Penguin Group (USA) Inc. Registered in U.S. Patent
and Trademark Office. Published simultaneously in Canada. Printed in Singapore.

Library of Congress Control Number: 90-80383   ISBN 978-0-448-40071-6   31

Chug, chug, chug. Puff, puff, puff. Ding-dong, ding-dong. The little train rumbled over the tracks. She was a happy little train for she had such a jolly load to carry. Her cars were filled full of good things for boys and girls.

There were toy animals—giraffes with long necks, Teddy

bears with almost no necks at all, and even a baby elephant. Then there were dolls—dolls with blue eyes and yellow curls, dolls with brown eyes and brown bobbed heads, and the funniest little toy clown you ever saw. And there were cars full of toy engines, airplanes, tops, jack-knives, picture puzzles, books, and every kind of thing boys or girls could want.

But that was not all. Some of the cars were filled with all sorts of good things for boys and girls to eat—big golden oranges, red-cheeked apples, bottles of creamy milk for their breakfasts, fresh spinach for their dinners, peppermint drops, and lollypops for after-meal treats.

The little train was carrying all these wonderful things to the good little boys and girls on the other side of the mountain. She puffed along merrily. Then all of a sudden she stopped with a jerk. She simply could not go another inch. She tried and she tried, but her wheels would not turn.

What were all those good little boys and girls on the other side of the mountain going to do without the wonderful toys to play with and the good food to eat?

"Here comes a shiny new engine," said the funny little clown who jumped out of the train. "Let us ask him to help us."

So all the dolls and toys cried out together:

"Please, Shiny New Engine, won't you please pull our train over the mountain? Our engine has broken down, and the boys

and girls on the other side won't have any toys to play with or
good food to eat unless you help us."

But the Shiny New Engine snorted: "I pull you? I am a Passenger Engine. I have just carried a fine big train over the mountain, with more cars than you ever dreamed of. My train had sleeping cars, with comfortable berths; a dining-car where waiters bring whatever hungry people want to eat; and parlor cars in which people sit in soft arm-chairs and look out of big plate-glass windows. I pull the likes of you? Indeed not!" And off he steamed to the roundhouse, where engines live when they are not busy.

How sad the little train and all the dolls and toys felt!
Then the little clown called out, "The Passenger Engine is not

the only one in the world. Here is another engine coming, a great big strong one. Let us ask him to help us."

The little toy clown waved his flag and the big strong engine came to a stop.

"Please, oh, please, Big Engine," cried all the dolls and toys together. "Won't you please pull our train over the mountain? Our engine has broken down, and the good little boys and girls on the other side won't have any toys to play with or good food to eat unless you help us."

But the Big Strong Engine bellowed: "I am a Freight Engine.

I have just pulled a big train loaded with big machines over the mountain. These machines print books and newspapers for grown-ups to read. I am a very important engine indeed. I won't pull the likes of you!" And the Freight Engine puffed off indignantly to the roundhouse.

The little train and all the dolls and toys were very sad.

"Cheer up," cried the little toy clown. "The Freight Engine is not the only one in the world. Here comes another. He looks very old and tired, but our train is so little, perhaps he can help us."

So the little toy clown waved his flag and the dingy, rusty old engine stopped.

"Please, Kind Engine," cried all the dolls and toys together. "Won't you please pull our train over the mountain? Our engine has broken down, and the boys and girls on the other side won't have any toys to play with or good food to eat unless you help us."

But the Rusty Old Engine sighed: "I am so tired. I must rest my weary wheels. I cannot pull even so little a train as yours over the mountain. I can not. I can not. I can not."

And off he rumbled to the roundhouse chugging, "I can not. I can not. I can not."

Then indeed the little train was very, very sad, and the dolls and toys were ready to cry.

But the little clown called out, "Here is another engine

coming, a little blue engine, a very little one, maybe she will help us."

The very little engine came chug, chugging merrily along. When she saw the toy clown's flag, she stopped quickly.

"What is the matter, my friends?" she asked kindly.

"Oh, Little Blue Engine," cried the dolls and toys. "Will you pull us over the mountain? Our engine has broken down and the good boys and girls on the other side won't have any toys to play with or good food to eat, unless you help us. Please, please, help us, Little Blue Engine."

"I'm not very big," said the Little Blue Engine. "They use me only for switching trains in the yard. I have never been over the mountain."

"But we must get over the mountain before the children awake," said all the dolls and the toys.

The very little engine looked up and saw the tears in the dolls' eyes. And she thought of the good little boys and girls on the other side of the mountain who would not have any toys or good food unless she helped.

Then she said, "I think I can. I think I can. I think I can." And she hitched herself to the little train.

She tugged and pulled and pulled and tugged and slowly,

slowly, slowly they started off.

The toy clown jumped aboard and all the dolls and the toy animals began to smile and cheer.

Puff, puff, chug, chug, went the Little Blue Engine. "I think I can—I think I can—I think I can—I think I can—I think I can—

I think I can—I think I can—I think I can—I think I can."

Up, up, up. Faster and faster and faster and faster the little engine climbed, until at last they reached the top of the mountain.

Down in the valley lay the city.

"Hurray, hurray," cried the funny little clown and all the dolls and toys. "The good little boys and girls in the city will be happy because you helped us, kind, Little Blue Engine."

And the Little Blue Engine smiled and seemed to say as she puffed steadily down the mountain. . .

"I thought I could. I thought I could. I thought I could.
I thought I could.

I thought I could.

I thought I could."